JUMP

DAVID McPHAIL

I Like to Read®

HOLIDAY HOUSE • NEW YORK

I Like to Read® books, created by award-winning
picture book artists as well as talented newcomers,
instill confidence and the joy of reading in new readers.

We want to hear every new reader say, **"I like to read!"**

Visit our website for flash cards, activities, and more about the series:
www.holidayhouse.com/ILiketoRead
#ILTR
This book has been tested by an educational expert
and determined to be a guided reading level A.

I LIKE TO READ is a registered trademark of Holiday House Publishing, Inc.

Copyright © 2018 by David McPhail
All Rights Reserved
HOLIDAY HOUSE is registered in the U.S. Patent and Trademark Office.
Printed and bound in September 2018 at Tien Wah Press, Johor Bahru, Johor, Malaysia.
The artwork was created with pen and ink and watercolor.
www.holidayhouse.com
First Edition
3 5 7 9 10 8 6 4

Library of Congress Cataloging-in-Publication Data

Names: McPhail, David, 1940- author, illustrator.
Title: Jump / David McPhail.
Description: First edition. | New York : Holiday House, [2018] |
Series: I like to read | Summary: "Two boys and a frog, a cow, and other animals
jump for joy in this easy-to-read book"—Provided by publisher.
Identifiers: LCCN 2017003462| ISBN 9780823438891 (hardcover) | ISBN 9780823438914 (paperback)
Subjects: | CYAC: Jumping—Fiction. | Animals—Fiction.
Classification: LCC PZ7.M478818 Jum 2018 | DDC [E]—dc23 LC record available at https://lccn.loc.gov/2017003462

To My Darlin' Avery

I can jump.

She can jump.

We can jump.

A bug can jump.

A frog can jump.

A rabbit can jump.

A kangaroo can jump.

A cow can jump.

A hippo can jump.

We can jump.

You can jump.